the
one in
the middle
is the
green kangaroo

the
one in
the middle
is the
green kangaroo

JUDY BLUME

illustrations by Debbie Ridpath Ohi

A Richard Jackson Book
Atheneum Books for Young Readers
New York London Toronto Sydney New Delhi

Books by Judy Blume

YOUNG ADULT AND MIDDLE GRADE

Are You There God? It's Me, Margaret.

Blubber

Deenie

Forever . . .

Here's to You, Rachel Robinson

Iggie's House

It's Not the End of the World

Just as Long as We're Together

Letters to Judy: What Kids Wish They Could Tell You

Places I Never Meant to Be: Original Stories by Censored Writers
(edited by Judy Blume)

Starring Sally J. Freedman as Herself

Then Again, Maybe I Won't

Tiger Eyes

THE FUDGE BOOKS

Tales of a Fourth Grade Nothing

Otherwise Known as Sheila the Great

Superfudge

Fudge-a-mania

Double Fudge

PICTURE BOOKS AND STORYBOOKS

The Pain and the Great One

Freckle Juice

The Pain and the Great One series

Soupy Saturdays

Cool Zone

Going, Going, Gone!

Friend or Fiend?

ATHENEUM BOOKS FOR YOUNG READERS
An imprint of Simon & Schuster Children's Publishing Division
1230 Avenue of the Americas, New York, New York 10020
This book is a work of fiction. Any references to historical events,
real people, or real places are used fictitiously. Other names, characters, places,
and events are products of the author's imagination, and any resemblance to
actual events or places or persons, living or dead, is entirely coincidental.
Text copyright © 1981 by Judy Blume
Illustrations copyright © 2014 by Debbie Ridpath Ohi
All rights reserved, including the right of reproduction
in whole or in part in any form.
ATHENEUM BOOKS FOR YOUNG READERS is a registered
trademark of Simon & Schuster, Inc.
Atheneum logo is a trademark of Simon & Schuster, Inc.
For information about special discounts for bulk purchases, please contact Simon &
Schuster Special Sales at 1-866-506-1949 or business@simonandschuster.com.
The Simon & Schuster Speakers Bureau can bring authors to your live event.
For more information or to book an event, contact the Simon & Schuster Speakers
Bureau at 1-866-248-3049 or visit our website at www.simonspeakers.com.
Also available in an Atheneum Books for Young Readers hardcover edition
Book design by Tom Daly
The text for this book is set in New Century Schoolbook LT Std.
The illustrations for this book are digitally rendered.
Manufactured in the United States of America
0616 OFF
First Atheneum Books for Young Readers paperback edition May 2014
4 6 8 10 9 7 5 3
Library of Congress Cataloging-in-Publication Data
Blume, Judy.
The one in the middle is the green kangaroo / Judy Blume ; illustrated by Debbie
Ridpath Ohi.
pages cm
Originally published in a different form by Reilly & Lee in 1969.
Summary: Second-grader Freddy hates being the middle one in the family until he
gets a part in the school play.
ISBN 978-1-4814-1132-5 (hardcover)
ISBN 978-1-4814-1131-8 (paperback)
[1. Middle-born children—Fiction. 2. Brothers and sisters—Fiction. 3. Family life—
Fiction. 4. Schools—Fiction. 5. Theater—Fiction. 6. Humorous stories.] I. Ohi, Debbie
Ridpath, 1962– illustrator. II. Title.
PZ7.B6265On 2014
[Fic]—dc23   2014007152

This title was previously published in a slightly different form.

For Randy and Larry,
who have been there from the beginning
—J. B.

For Ginger, who helped me find my voice
—D. R. O.

Freddy Dissel had two problems. One was his older brother Mike. The other was his younger sister Ellen. Freddy thought a lot about being the one in the middle. But there was nothing he could do about it. He felt like the peanut butter part of a sandwich, squeezed between Mike and Ellen.

Every year Mike got new clothes. He grew too big for his old ones. But Mike's old clothes weren't too small for Freddy. They fit him just fine.

Freddy used to have a room of his own. That was before Ellen was born. Now Ellen had a room of *her* own. Freddy moved in with Mike. Mom and Dad said, "It's the boys' room." But they couldn't fool Freddy. He knew better!

Once, Freddy tried to join Mike and his friends. But Mike said, "Get out of the way, kid!" So Freddy tried

to play with Ellen. Ellen didn't understand how to play his way. She messed up all of Freddy's things. Freddy got mad and pinched her. Ellen screamed.

"Freddy Dissel!" Mom yelled. "You shouldn't be mean to Ellen. She's smaller than you. She's just a baby!"

Ellen didn't look like a baby to Freddy. She didn't sound like a baby either. She even goes to nursery school, Freddy thought. *Some baby!*

Freddy figured things would never get better for him. He would always be a great big middle nothing!

Rehearsal for Grade 5 and 6 SCHOOL PLAY tonight!

Then one day Freddy heard about the school play. Mike had never been in a play. Ellen had never been in a play. This was his chance to do something special. Freddy decided he would try it.

He waited two whole days before he went to his teacher. "Ms. Gumber," he said. "I want to be in the school play."

Ms. Gumber smiled and shook her head. "I'm sorry, Freddy," she said. "The play is being done by the fifth and sixth graders. The big boys and girls, like Mike."

Freddy looked at the floor and mumbled. "That figures!" He started to walk away.

"Wait a minute, Freddy," Ms. Gumber called. "I'll talk to Ms. Matson anyway. She's in charge of the play. I'll find out if they need any second graders to help."

Finally, Ms. Gumber told Freddy that Ms. Matson needed someone to play a special part. Ms. Gumber said, "Go to the auditorium this afternoon. Maybe you'll get the part."

"Great!" Freddy hollered.

Later he went to the auditorium. Ms. Matson was waiting for him. Freddy walked right up close to her. He said, "I want to be in the play."

Ms. Matson asked him to go up on the stage and say that again—in a very loud voice.

Freddy had never been on a stage.
It was big. It made him feel small.
He looked out at Ms. Matson.

"I AM FREDDY!" he shouted. "I WANT TO BE IN THE PLAY."

"Good," Ms. Matson called. "Now then Freddy, can you jump?"

What kind of question was that, Freddy wondered. Of course he could jump. He was in second grade, wasn't he? So he jumped. He jumped all around the stage—big jumps and little jumps. When he was through, Ms. Matson clapped her hands, and Freddy climbed down from the stage.

"I think you will be fine as the Green Kangaroo, Freddy," Ms. Matson said. "It's a very important part."

Freddy didn't tell anyone at home

about the play until dinnertime. Then he said, "Guess what, every- one? Guess what I'm going to be?"

No one paid any attention to what

Freddy was saying. They were too busy eating.

"I'm going to be in a play," Freddy said. "I'm going to be the Green Kangaroo!"

Mike choked on his potato and knocked over a whole glass of milk. Ellen laughed because Mike spilled his milk. Dad jumped up. He patted Mike on the back to make him stop choking.

Mom ran to get the sponge. She cleaned up the spilled milk. Freddy just sat there and smiled.

"What did you say?" Mike asked.

"I *said* I'm going to be in the school play. I *said* I'm going to be the Green Kangaroo!"

"It can't be true," Mike yelled. "Why would they pick you?"

"Because I can jump," Freddy said.

"I can jump, too," Ellen said.

"*Everybody* can jump," Mike told them.

"Yes, but not like me," Freddy said. "And besides, I can talk loud."

"I can talk loud," Ellen said. "Listen to this." And she screamed. "See how loud I can talk."

"That's enough, Ellen," Mom said.

Dad said, "Freddy, I think it's wonderful that you got the part in the play."

Mom kissed him and said, "We're all proud of you, Freddy."

Ellen laughed. "Green Kangaroo,

Green Kangaroo," she said over and over again.

Mike just shook his head and said, "I still can't believe it. *He's* going to be the Green Kangaroo."

"It's true," Freddy said. "Just me. All by myself—the only Green Kangaroo in the play."

3

The next two weeks were busy ones for Freddy. He had to practice being the Green Kangaroo a lot. He practiced at school on the stage. He practiced at home, too. He made kangaroo faces in front of the mirror. He did kangaroo jumps on his bed. He even dreamed about Green Kangaroos at night.

Finally, the day of the play came. The whole family would

be there. Some of their neighbors were coming, too.

Mom hugged Freddy extra hard as he left for school. "We'll be there watching you, Green Kangaroo," she said.

After lunch Ms. Gumber called to Freddy. "Time to go now. Time to get into your costume." Ms. Gumber walked to the hall with Freddy.

Then she whispered, "We'll be in the second row. Break a leg."

"Break a leg?" Freddy said.

Ms. Gumber laughed. "That means good luck when you're in a play."

"Oh," Freddy said. "I thought you meant I should fall off the stage and *really* break a leg."

Ms. Gumber laughed again. She ruffled Freddy's hair.

Freddy went to Ms. Matson's room. The girls in the sixth grade had made his costume. They all giggled when Ms. Matson helped Freddy into it. His Green Kangaroo

suit covered all of him. It even had
green feet. Only his face stuck out.
Ms. Matson put some green dots on
it. "We'll wash them off later. Okay?"

"Okay," Freddy mumbled. He
jumped over to the mirror. He looked
at himself. He really felt like a
Green Kangaroo.

It was time for the play to begin. Freddy waited backstage with the fifth and

sixth graders who were in the play. They looked at him and smiled. He tried to smile back. But the smile wouldn't come. His heart started to beat faster. His stomach bounced up and down. He felt funny. Then Ms. Matson leaned close to him. She said, "They're waiting for you, Freddy. Go ahead."

He jumped out onto the stage. He looked out into the audience. All those people were down there—somewhere. He knew they were. It was very quiet. He could hear his heart. He thought he saw Mom and Dad. He thought he saw Ellen. He thought he saw Mike and Ms. Gumber and his second grade class and all of his neighbors,

too. They were all out there somewhere. They were all in the middle of
the audience. But Freddy wasn't in
the middle. He was all by himself up
on the stage. He had a job to do. He
had to be the Green Kangaroo.

Freddy smiled. His heart slowed
down. His stomach stayed still. He
felt better. He smiled a bigger, wider
smile. He felt good.

"HELLO EVERYONE," Freddy
said. "I AM THE GREEN KANGA-
ROO. WELCOME."

The play began. Freddy did his
big and little jumps. Every few min-
utes one of the fifth or sixth graders
in the play said to him, "And who
are you?"

Freddy jumped around and answered. "Me? I am the Green Kangaroo!" It was easy. That was all he had to say. It was fun, too. Every time he said it the audience laughed. Freddy liked it when they laughed. It was a funny play.

When it was all over everyone on the stage took a bow. Then Ms. Matson came out and waited for the

audience to get quiet. She said, "A special thank-you to our second grader, Freddy Dissel. He played the part of the Green Kangaroo."

Freddy jumped over to the middle of the stage. He took a big, low bow all by himself. The audience clapped hard for a long time.

4

Freddy didn't care much about wearing Mike's clothes anymore. He didn't care much about sharing Mike's room either. He didn't care much that Ellen was small and cute. He didn't even care much about being the one in the middle. He felt just great being Freddy Dissel.

ALL OF THE QUESTIONS.
ALL OF THE ANSWERS.

Judy Blume has a whole new look!
Which one will you read first?